KT-592-029

Contents

In this decayed hole among the mountains
In the faint moonlight, the grass is singing
Over the tumbled graves, about the chapel
There is the empty chapel, onlty the wind's home.
It has no windows, and the door swings,
Dry bones can harm no one.
Only a cock stood on the rooftree
Co co rico co co rico
In a flash of lightning. Then a damp gust
Bringing rain

From *The Waste Land* by T. S. ELIOT,
Faber and Faber Ltd

The Grass is Singing

DORIS LESSING

Level 5

Retold by Andy Hopkins and Jocelyn Potter
Series Editors: Andy Hopkins and Jocelyn Potter

Pearson Education Limited
Edinburgh Gate, Harlow,
Essex CM20 2JE, England
and Associated Companies throughout the world.

ISBN 0 582 41789 9

The Grass is Singing by Doris Lessing
Copyright © 1950 by Doris Lessing
This adaptation first published by Penguin Books 1992
Published by Addison Wesley Longman Limited and Penguin Books Ltd. 1998
New edition first published 1999

Third impression 2000

Text copyright © Andy Hopkins and Jocelyn Potter 1992
Illustrations copyright © David Cuzik 1992
All rights reserved

Acknowledgements
The publishers wish to make grateful acknowledgement to the following
for permission to reproduce copyright material: page vi, Faber and Faber.
Every effort has been made to trace copyright holders in every case. The
publishers would be interested to hear from any not acknowledged here

Typeset by RefineCatch Limited, Bungay, Suffolk
Set in 11/14pt Monotype Bembo
Printed in Spain by Mateu Cromo, S.A. Pinto (Madrid)

Published by Pearson Education Limited in association with
Penguin Books Ltd., both companies being subsidiaries of Pearson Plc

For a complete list of the titles available in the Penguin Readers series please write to your local
Pearson Education office or to: Marketing Department, Penguin Longman Publishing,
5 Bentinck Street, London W1M 5RN.

Introduction

How had all this started? What sort of woman had Mary Turner been before she came to the farm and had been driven slowly crazy by heat, loneliness and poverty? He tried to think clearly, to get a picture of what had really happened.

In southern Africa in the 1940s, the whites are in control. They control through fear — and they must stay in control. So when a white woman is murdered by her black servant all the whites agree: the law must take its course. The case must be simple and quick — without too many questions.

But there *are* questions, and soon people start asking them. How did Mary Turner lose control? *Why* did the servant murder her? How could a servant even *think* of it?

The answers are not simple. They are as difficult and painful as Mary Turner's life itself — a life in a place where she was never meant to be . . .

Doris Lessing was born in Kermanshah, Iran in 1919, the daughter of British parents. The family moved to Rhodesia (now Zimbabwe) when she was five and she was brought up on a farm there. After marrying — and divorcing — twice, she became involved with a political group who were demanding greater freedom for black people. The Rhodesian government sent her out of the country in 1949 and she moved to London. She had with her the pages of her first novel, *The Grass is Singing*, which was very successful and came out in the USA, UK and ten other European countries at the same time. After this, she supported herself and her son by writing.

Doris Lessing has written many different kinds of stories and novels. Many are based on her experiences in Africa. She has won many prizes for her books.

Chapter 1   A Bad Business

MURDER MYSTERY

by Special Reporter

Mary Turner, wife of Richard Turner, a farmer at Ngesi, was found dead at her home yesterday morning. The houseboy has admitted killing her. It is believed that theft was the reason behind the murder.

The newspaper did not say much. People all over the country must have read the short report and felt angry – and yet satisfied, as if their strong beliefs about the natives had been proved correct. When natives steal, murder or attack women, that is the feeling white people have. And then they turned the page to read something else.

The people who knew the Turners did not turn the page so quickly. Many must have cut out the report, keeping it perhaps as a warning. However, they did not discuss the murder. Although the three people in a position to explain the facts said nothing, everyone seemed to know by some sixth sense what had really happened. 'A bad business,' someone remarked each time the subject was mentioned. 'A very bad business,' came the reply. And that was all that was said. There seemed to be general unspoken agreement that the Turner case should be forgotten as soon as possible.

In this country area, white farming families lived at great distances from each other and met only occasionally. They were usually grateful for something to talk about, but the murder was not discussed. To an outsider it seemed perhaps as if Charles Slatter had told people to keep quiet, but in fact he had not. The steps he had taken were not part of any plan; he had just done what came naturally.

Nobody liked the Turners, although few of their neighbours had ever actually met them. They 'kept themselves to themselves', never attended any social events, and lived in that awful little box house. How could they live like that? Some natives had houses as good; and it gave a bad impression for them to see whites living in such a way. The Turners were not just poor whites; they were, after all, British!

The more one thinks about it, the more extraordinary the whole matter becomes. Not the murder itself, but the way people felt about it; the way they pitied Dick Turner, as if his wife Mary were something unpleasant and unclean. It was almost as if people felt that she deserved such a death. But they did not ask any questions.

They must have wondered who that 'special reporter' was. It can only really have been Charlie Slatter, since he knew more about the Turners than anyone else, and was at the farm on the day of the murder. He appeared to take control, and people felt that to be quite reasonable. He was one of them, and why should anyone else be allowed to interfere in the business of white farmers? And it was Charlie Slatter who arranged everything so that the whole matter was cleared up cleanly and quickly.

Slatter lived five miles from the Turners. The farm boys came to him first when they discovered the body, and he sent a message to Sergeant Denham at the police station, twelve miles away. The police did not have to search far for the murderer when they reached Turners' farm; after walking through the house and examining the body, they moved to the area outside the front of the building and, as soon as he saw them, Moses stood up, walked towards them and said: 'Here I am.' They tied his hands and took him back towards the house. In the distance they could see Dick

Turner moving around in the bush, talking crazily to himself, his hands full of earth and leaves. They left him alone. Although he looked mad, he was a white man; black men, even policemen, do not lay hands on white skin.

Some people did wonder for a moment why the native had allowed the police to catch him. Why did he not at least try and escape? But this question was soon forgotten.

So Charlie Slatter had sent the message to the police station, and then driven at great speed to the Turners' place in his fat American car. Who was Charlie Slatter? He started his working life as a shop assistant in London and was still a Londoner after twenty years in Africa. He had come to Africa for one reason . . . to make money. He made it. He made a lot. He was a hard man, but was sometimes generous when he wanted to be. He was hard with his wife and children until he made money; then they got everything they wanted. Above all, he was hard with his workers, for Slatter believed in farming with a whip. He had once killed a native worker with one in sudden anger and had had to pay a fine of thirty pounds. Since then he had kept his temper. It was he who had told Dick Turner that a farmer should buy a whip before any other piece of farm equipment. But the whip did not do the Turners any good, as we shall see.

While Slatter drove as fast as he could to the Turners' place, he wondered why Marston had not come to him about the murder. Marston was Turner's assistant, but was after all employed by Slatter. Why had he not sent a note? Where was he? The hut he lived in was only a few hundred yards away from the house itself. But, thought Charlie, anything was possible with this particular Englishman, with his soft face and voice and good manners.

On the way, Slatter had to stop to repair two flat tyres, but he finally reached the house. The policemen were standing with Moses outside the house. Moses was a great powerful man with deep black skin, dressed in a vest and shorts which were wet and muddy. Charlie walked towards him and looked directly into his face. The man looked back without expression. For a moment Charlie's face showed fear. Why fear? Moses was as good as dead already, wasn't he? But Charlie was worried, uncertain. Then he recovered and turned away.

'Turner!' he called. Close by now, Dick turned but did not seem to know him. Charlie took him by the arm and led him to the car. He did not yet know that Dick was insane. After helping him into the back seat, he went into the house and found Marston.

'Where were you?' asked Charlie at once.

'I slept late this morning,' Marston said. The fear in his voice was not Charlie's fear, but a simple fear of death. 'I found Mrs Turner just outside the front door when I came to the house. Then the policemen came. I was expecting you.'

Charlie went into the bedroom. Mary Turner lay under a dirty white sheet. He stared at her with an anger and hatred that is hard for us to understand. Then, with a sudden movement, he turned and left the room.

'I moved her inside on to the bed, away from the dogs,' explained Marston. 'There was blood everywhere. I cleaned it up . . . perhaps that was wrong of me.'

Charlie sat down and looked at the assistant carefully. 'What do *you* know about all this?' he asked, after a silence.

Marston hesitated. 'I don't know. Nothing really. It's all so difficult . . .'

Charlie examined the young man. Another soft boy with a private education who had come to Africa to learn to be a farmer. They were all so similar. They usually came with ideas of equality, and were often shocked at first by the way whites behaved towards the natives. A few months later these young men had become stronger and harder and learnt to accept the way things were. If Tony Marston had spent a few more months in the country it would have been easy. That was Charlie's feeling.

Charlie walked towards Moses and looked directly into his face.
The man looked back without expression. For a moment Charlie's
face showed fear.

'What do you mean, it's all so difficult?'

There was a warning in Charlie's voice, and Marston did not know what it meant. His ideas of right and wrong were becoming confused. He had his own ideas about the murder but he could not say them clearly. He felt the murder was logical enough after the events of the last few days. They could only end in something violent or ugly. But could he not say what he thought?

'Look,' said Charlie directly, 'have you any idea why this nigger* murdered Mrs Turner?'

'Yes, I have.'

'Well, we'd better leave it to the Sergeant then.'

Marston understood. Charlie was telling him to keep his mouth shut. He kept quiet, angry and confused.

Sergeant Denham arrived and the three of them went silently into the living room. Charlie Slatter and Denham stood opposite Marston, side by side like two judges. They knew each other well, of course.

'Bad business,' said the Sergeant briefly. He opened his notebook, and looked at Tony. 'I need to ask you a few questions,' he said. 'How long have you been here?'

'About three weeks.'

'Living in this house?'

'No, in a hut down the path.'

'You were going to run this place while they were away?'

'Yes, for six months. And then I intended to go and work on another farm.'

'When did you find out about this business?'

'They didn't call me. I woke and found Mrs Turner.'

Tony was becoming more angry and confused. Why were they questioning him like this? Why did he feel guilty?

'You had your meals with the Turners?'

* *Nigger*: an unacceptable word used by whites to refer to black people. Black people are extremely offended by this word.

'Yes.'

'Other than that, did you spend much time with them?'

'No, only at work. I've been busy learning my job.'

'Were you friendly with Turner?'

'Yes, I think so. He was not easy to know. He was always working. Of course he was very unhappy about leaving the place.' He looked at Charlie; Charlie had been responsible for making Dick leave the farm.

Denham shut his book and paused. There was a silence in the room. It was as if they all knew that what happened next would be of great importance. For a moment fear crossed Charlie's face.

'Did you see anything unusual while you were here?' he asked Tony.

'Yes, I did,' Tony burst out, knowing now that they wanted to stop him telling the truth.

They both looked at him in surprise.

'Look,' he said, 'I'll tell you what I know from the beginning . . .'

'You mean you know why Mrs Turner was murdered?' asked the Sergeant.

'No. But I have some ideas.'

'Ideas? We don't want ideas. We want facts. Anyway, remember Dick Turner. This is most unpleasant for him.'

Tony was trying to control his anger. 'Do you or do you not want to hear what I have to say?'

'Of course. But we *only* want facts . . . we're not interested in what you think might have happened. So give me any facts you have.'

'But you know I don't have facts. This is not a simple matter.'

'Tell me, for instance . . . how did Mrs Turner treat this house-boy?' continued the Sergeant.

'Badly, I thought,' replied Tony.

'Yes, well, that's not unusual in this country, is it?'

'Needs a man to know how to handle these boys. A woman always gets it wrong,' added Charlie Slatter.

'Look here . . .' began Tony. But he stopped when he saw their faces. For they had both turned to look at him, and there was no doubt that this was the final warning. He wanted to speak but he was too angry and confused to continue.

'Let's get her out of here,' suggested Charlie.' It's getting hot.'

As the policemen moved Mary's stiff body from the house to the car, Denham said, as if talking to himself, 'This is all quite simple. There are no unusual circumstances.' He looked at Tony.

Moses' face showed no feelings as he was taken away. The police car drove off through the trees, followed by Charlie Slatter and Dick Turner. Tony found himself standing alone in the silence of the empty farm. He turned to look at the house, with its bare tin roof and its dusty brick floor covered with animal skins. How could they have lived in such a place for so long? The heat inside was terrible.

How had all this started? What sort of woman had Mary Turner been before she came to the farm and had been driven slowly crazy by heat, loneliness and poverty? He tried to think clearly, to get a picture of what had really happened. But it was too hot, and those two men had warned him – not by words but by looks. What were they warning him about? He thought he understood now. The anger he had seen in Charlie Slatter's face was 'white society' fighting to defend itself. And that 'white society' could never, ever admit that a white person, and particularly a white woman, can have a human relationship, good or evil, with a black person. For as soon as it admits that, it falls.

'I'm getting out of this place,' he told himself. 'I am going to the other end of the country. Let the Slatters do as they like. What's it got to do with me?' That morning, he packed his things and went to tell Charlie he was leaving. Charlie seemed not to care. After all, there was no need for a manager on Dick Turner's land now that Dick would not come back.

Tony went back into town and tried to find work on another farm. He tried a few jobs but was unable to settle in one place. When the trial came, he said what was expected of him. It was suggested that the native had murdered Mary Turner while drunk, in search of money and jewellery.

After the trial, Tony left for Northern Rhodesia. Before long he found himself working in an office, doing the paperwork that he had come to Africa to avoid. But it wasn't so bad really. Life is never as one expects it to be, after all.

Chapter 2　Two Lonely People

As the railway spread all over Southern Africa, small groups of buildings grew up every few miles along the lines. There was the station, the post office, sometimes a hotel, but always a shop.

For Mary, the shop was the real centre of her life, even more important to her than to most children. She was always running across to bring some dried fruit or some tinned fish for her mother, or to find out if the weekly newspaper had arrived. And she would stay there for hours, staring at the piles of sticky coloured sweets, looking at the little Greek girl whom she was not allowed to play with. And later, when she grew older, it was the place her father bought his drink; the place he spent his evenings. And of course it was from the shop that the monthly bills for food and her father's drink came. Every month her parents argued, and they never had enough money to meet the bills. But life went on.

When Mary was sent away to school, her life changed. The village, with its dust and chickens and the coughing of trains, seemed another, empty world. She was extremely happy at school, and did not look forward to going home in the holidays.

At sixteen she left school and took a job as a secretary in an office in town. Four years later, by the time her mother died, she had a comfortable life with her own friends and a good job. From that time until his own death when she was twenty-five, she did not see her father; they did not even write to each other. But being alone in the world held no terrors for Mary. In fact, she liked it. And she loved the town; she felt safe there. She was at her prettiest then – rather thin, with a curtain of light-brown hair, serious blue eyes, and fashionable clothes.

By thirty, nothing had changed. Indeed, she felt a little surprised that she had reached such an age, for she felt no different from when she was sixteen. All this time, Mary had lived in a girls' club. She chose it at first because it reminded her of the school where she had been so happy. She liked the crowds of girls, and eating in the big dining-room, and coming home after the cinema to find a friend in her room waiting to talk to her.

Outside the girls' club she had a very full and active life, although she was not the kind of woman who is the centre of a crowd. She had lots of men friends who took her out and treated her like a sister. She played hockey and tennis with them, swam, went to parties and dances. The years passed. Her friends married one by one, but she continued in much the same way, dressing and wearing her hair just as she had done when she left school.

She seemed not to care for men. She spent all her time outside work with them, but did not feel she depended on them in any way. She listened to the other girls' men problems with interest and amazement, for she had no such problems. Then, one day, while sitting outside a friend's house, she heard people talking about her through an open window.

'She's not fifteen any longer. Someone should tell her about her clothes.'

'How old is she?'

'Must be over thirty. She was working long before I was, and that was over twelve years ago.'

'Why doesn't she marry? Surely she's had plenty of chances.'

There was a dry laugh. 'I don't think so. My husband liked her once, but he thinks she'll never marry. She just isn't like that.'

'Oh come on! She'd make someone a good wife.'

'She should marry someone much older than herself. A man of fifty would suit her . . . you'll see, she'll marry someone old enough to be her father one of these days.'

Mary could hardly believe the way these 'friends' had talked about her. She sat in her room for hour after hour, thinking. 'Why did they say those things? What's the matter with me?' But she began to look at herself more carefully. She changed her hair style and began wearing suits to work, although they made her feel uncomfortable. And she started looking around for someone to marry.

The first man to approach her was fifty-five years old, with half-grown children; his wife had died a few years earlier. She felt safe with him, because he seemed to know what he wanted: a friend, a mother for his children and someone to look after his house. Everything went well until she accepted his offer of marriage. That evening he tried to kiss her for the first time, and as he touched her she realised that she felt disgusted to have him so close to her. She ran from his house back to the club, fell on her bed and cried.

From that evening, and despite her own age, she avoided men over thirty. She did not know it, but her friends laughed behind her back when they heard the story of her running from the man. She was beginning to be afraid to go out. And then she met Dick Turner. It could have been anybody — or rather, anybody who treated her as if she were wonderful and special. She needed that badly.

They met by chance at a cinema. Dick rarely came to town, except when he had to buy goods for the farm. He disliked its suburbs full of ugly little houses that seemed to have nothing to do with the African land and the huge blue sky. The fashionable shops and expensive restaurants made him feel uncomfortable, so he

Suddenly Dick noticed a woman sitting near them, the light from the film shining on her eyes and her fair hair.

always escaped as soon as possible back to his farm, where he felt at home.

Above all, Dick Turner hated the cinema. A friend had persuaded him to go, but when he found himself inside he could not keep his eyes on the film. The story seemed to have no meaning and it bored him. It was hot and sticky in the cinema. So after a while he gave up looking at the film and turned his attention to the audience. Suddenly he noticed a woman sitting near them, the light from the film shining on her eyes and her fair hair.

'Who's that?' he asked.

His friend looked over to where he was pointing. 'That's Mary.'

Dick stared at her hair and her lovely face. The next day he returned to his farm, but he could not stop thinking about the girl called Mary.

Dick had of course long ago forbidden himself to think about women. He had started farming five years before and was still not making money. He had heavy debts, and had given up drink and cigarettes. He worked all the hours of the day, taking his meals on the farm; the farm was his whole life. His dream was to marry and have children, but he could not ask any woman to share such a life. Not until he could afford to build a new house and pay for some small luxuries.

But now he found himself thinking all the time about the girl in the cinema. About a month after the last visit, he set off on another visit to town, although it was not really necessary. He did his business quickly and then went off in search of someone who could tell him Mary's surname.

When he finally found the club, he failed to recognise Mary. He saw a tall, thin girl with deep blue eyes that looked hurt. Her hair was pulled tightly across her head. She wore trousers. He was quite an old-fashioned man in many ways, and he did not feel comfortable with women wearing trousers.

'Are you looking for me?' she asked in a shy voice.

He was so disappointed at the way she looked that he found it difficult to speak, but when he found his voice he asked her to go for a drive. As the evening went on, he began to find in her again the woman he had seen at the cinema. He wanted to love her. He needed someone to love and when he left her that night it was with regret, saying he would come again.

Back on the farm he told himself he was a fool. He could not continue to see her. He could not ask a woman to spend her life with him on this farm. For two months he worked hard and tried to put Mary out of his mind.

For Mary, these two months were a terrible dream. He had decided not to come back; her friends were right, there was something wrong with her. But still she hoped. She stopped going out in the evenings, and sat in her room waiting for him to call. Her

13

employer told her to take a holiday because she could not keep her mind on her work. Yet what was Dick to her? Nothing. She hardly knew him.

Weeks after she had given up hope, Dick arrived at her door. She managed with great difficulty to greet him calmly, and she still appeared calm as he asked her to marry him. He was grateful when she accepted, and they were married two weeks later. Her desire to get married so quickly surprised him; he saw her as a busy and popular woman and thought it would take her time to arrange things. Indeed, this idea of her was partly what made her attractive to him. But a quick marriage was fine with him. He explained that he was too poor to afford a holiday, and so after the wedding they went straight to the farm.

Chapter 3   A New Life

It was late at night by the time they arrived. The car came to a stop and Mary woke up. Dick got out and went to fetch a light. She looked around her. The moon had gone behind a cloud and it was suddenly quite dark. The air was full of strange sounds and smells. Mary saw a small, square building with a metal roof, surrounded by low trees. Then she saw a light at the window, and Dick appeared carrying a candle. Mary entered the house. The room seemed tiny, and thrown across the brick floor were animal skins which gave the room a strong unpleasant smell. She knew Dick was watching her face for signs of disappointment so she forced herself to smile, but deep inside she was filled with horror. She had not expected this.

Mary felt protective towards Dick, though. He was shy and nervous, and this made her feel a little less nervous herself. When he brought tea and two cracked cups she was disgusted, but as she took the teapot from him and poured she began to feel she could have a place there. She felt him watching her, proud and delighted.

Mary saw a small, square building with a metal roof, surrounded
by low trees. Then Dick appeared carrying a candle.

Now that he had a wife, it seemed to Dick that he had been a
fool to wait so long. He told her all about his life on the farm: how
he had built the house with his own hands; how he had collected
each piece of furniture; how Charlie Slatter's wife had made the
heavy curtain that separated the living room from the bedroom. As
he spoke, she began to think of when she was a child – the poverty,
the emptiness, the problems her mother had. And now it seemed
she was back in that world, the world she had escaped from all those
years ago.

'Let's go next door,' she said suddenly. Dick got up, surprised
and a little hurt. Next door was the bedroom. There was a hanging
cupboard, some shelves, and some large boxes with a mirror
standing on top. In the middle of the room was the bed which

Dick had bought for their marriage, an old-fashioned bed, high and huge.

Seeing her standing there looking lost and confused, Dick left her alone to get ready for bed. As he took off his clothes in the next room he felt guilty again. He had had no right to marry, no right to bring her to this. Returning to the bedroom, he found her lying in bed with her back to him. He touched her gently and tenderly.

It was not so bad, Mary thought when it was all over. It meant nothing to her, nothing at all. Lack of involvement came naturally to her, and if Dick felt as if he had been denied then his sense of guilt told him that he deserved it. As he reached to turn out the light, he whispered to himself, 'I had no right . . . no right.' Mary fell asleep holding his hand protectively, as she might have held the hand of a sick child.

'Did you sleep well?' asked Dick, coming back into the bedroom the next morning.

'Yes, thank you.'

'Tea is coming now.' They were polite with each other.

An elderly native brought in the tea and put it on the table.

'This is the new missus,' Dick said to him. 'Mary, this is Samson. He'll look after you.'

After Dick had left to start his day's work, she got up and looked around the house. Samson was cleaning the living room and all the furniture was pushed into the middle, so she walked outside and round to the back of the house. It will be hot here, she thought, but how beautiful the colours are: the green of the trees and the gold of the grass shining in the sun. She entered the house from the back through the kitchen, and found Samson in the bedroom making the bed.

She had never had contact with natives before as an employer. She had been forbidden to speak to her mother's servants, and in the club she had been kind to the waiters; to her the 'native prob-lem' meant other women's complaints at tea parties. She was afraid of them of course, since every white woman in Southern Africa is taught to fear natives from a very early age. And now she had to face the problem of how to handle them. But Samson seemed pleasant, and she thought she would like him.

'Missus like to see the kitchen?' he asked.

He showed her where all the food was kept in large locked metal boxes. Between Samson and Dick there was a perfect understanding: Dick locked everything, but always put out more food than was needed for any meal. This extra food was then used by Samson, but he hoped for better things now that there was a woman in the house. He showed Mary how the oven worked, where the wood pile was, where the bedclothes were kept.

It was only seven in the morning and already her face and body were starting to get hot and sticky.

Dick returned for breakfast about half an hour later. He sat in silence through the meal. More problems on the farm; two pieces of equipment broken while he was away. Mary said nothing. This was all too strange for her.

Immediately after breakfast, Dick took his hat off the chair and went out again. Mary looked for a cook-book and took it to the kitchen. Then, when her cooking experiments were over, she sat down with a book on kitchen kaffir.* This was clearly the first thing she had to learn; Samson spoke little English, and she needed to make him understand her.

Chapter 4   Something to Fill the Time

At first Mary threw herself into improving the house. With her own money she bought what she needed to make curtains,

* *Kaffir:* here, the rather rude, unacceptable name used by whites to refer to the native language of the black people. White people in Southern Africa also rudely refer to black people as 'Kaffirs', which blacks find offensive.

bedclothes and some dresses for herself. Then she spent a little on new cups and plates. The house soon began to lose its air of poverty, and within a month there was nothing left to do. Dick was amazed and pleased by the changes.

She then looked around for something else to keep her busy, and for the next few months she sewed. Hour after hour she sat sewing designs on dresses, handkerchieves, bedclothes and curtains. She began early in the morning and worked until the sun went down. Then the sewing came to an end. For the next two weeks she painted the house – inside and out. The little white house shone brightly in the hot sun.

Mary found she was tired. She tried filling the time by reading the books she had brought with her from the town, books she had read a hundred times before but still loved. As she read them again now, it was difficult to understand what she had got from them before. They seemed to be without meaning in this new, strange life, so she packed them away again.

'Can't we have ceilings?' she asked Dick one day. 'This room is so hot under the metal roof.'

'It would cost so much. Perhaps next year, if we do well,' he replied.

Samson was not happy. This woman never laughed. She put out exactly the right amount of food for their meals, and never left any extra for him. She regularly accused him of stealing, and there were often arguments in the kitchen. Dick could not understand her anger; he had always expected Samson to take some food for himself. But Mary could not accept this, and when food went missing she reduced Samson's wages. One evening, Samson left his job, saying that he was needed by his family, and to Mary's amazement Dick was angry with her. He was sorry to see Samson go.

Another native came to the door asking for work. He was young and tall but nervous, for he had never been inside a white person's house before. Mary gave him a job, paying him lower wages than

Samson. The following day the new boy dropped a plate and she sent him away again.

The next boy was quite different. He was used to working for white women. Mary followed him around all the time, checking that his work was done well, always calling him back if she found anything that was not finished to her satisfaction. She felt she could not take her eyes off him; as soon as her back was turned he would steal something, she was sure of that.

Time passed, and the heat made her feel worse and worse. She began to take baths in the afternoon. The boy brought cans of water and, when she was sure he was out of the house, she took her clothes off and poured the water over herself.

Dick noticed that the water was disappearing fast. It was fetched twice a week, and it took two men and a pair of animals about an hour each time. When Mary told him what she was using the water for, he could hardly believe it. He shouted angrily at her about the money she was wasting, and for Mary this seemed too much. He had brought her here to this awful place, but she had not complained. And now he refused to allow her to wash when she wanted! They agreed in the end that she would fill the bath and use the same water for several days.

When Dick left, she went into the bathroom and stared down at the old bath. It was made of metal and set into the mud floor. Over the years it had become covered with dirt. When she used it she sat in the middle, trying to keep her body away from the sides, getting out as soon as she could. The next day, she called the boy and told him to clean every bit of dirt from the bath, to clean it until it shone. It was eleven o'clock.

When Dick returned for lunch he found her cooking.

'Why are you doing the cooking? Where's the boy?'

'Cleaning the bath,' she said angrily.

Dick went to the bathroom where the boy was still trying, with little success, to remove the dirt from the bath.

'Why make him do it now?' he said to Mary. 'It's been like that for years. It's not dirt in the bath – it just changes colour because it's made of metal. He'll never get it like you want it.'

But she insisted that the boy should continue, and Dick returned to the fields without eating. He could not be with her when she was like this. Mary sat on the sofa and listened. At half past three the boy walked into the living room and said he was going to have some food. She had forgotten completely about his need to eat; in fact she had never thought of natives as needing to eat at all.

When he had gone, she went outside. The week before, a fire had spread over part of their farm and still, here and there, fallen trees smoked in large areas of blackness where the fire had destroyed the crops. She tried not to think about the money they had lost.

Suddenly she saw a car in the distance, and a few minutes later she realised it was coming towards the house. Visitors! Dick had said she should expect people to call. She ran to get the boy to make tea, but of course he was not there. She rushed out to the old tree in front of the house and beat the piece of hanging metal ten times. This was the signal that the houseboy should come immediately. She looked down at her dress, but it was too late – the car was almost at the house. And then she saw Dick's car coming too, and was glad that he would be here to receive the visitors.

Charlie Slatter and his wife came in and sat down, the men on one side of the room and the women on the other. While the men talked about farming, Mrs Slatter tried to say kind things about what Mary had done to the house. And she meant them; she remembered what it was like to be poor. But Mary was ashamed and embarrassed by her surroundings, so became very stiff and uncomfortable and did not return Mrs Slatter's friendliness. After a while Mrs Slatter stopped trying, and the two talked with some difficulty for the rest of the visit. Mary was glad when they left, but Dick had enjoyed his men's talk with Charlie.

'You should go and visit her sometimes,' Dick said. 'You can take the car.'

'But I don't want to. I'm not lonely,' Mary replied.

At that moment the servant came to them, holding his contract of work. He wanted to leave; he was needed by his family. Mary immediately lost her temper, but Dick silenced her. The boy told Dick that he had been given no time to eat that day. He could not work like this. Dick told him that Mary was new to life in the country and did not know much about running a house yet. It would not happen again.

Mary could not believe what she was hearing. Dick was taking the servant's side against her!

'He's human like everybody else,' shouted Dick. 'He's got to eat. Why does this bath have to be done in one day?'

'It's my house. He's my boy. Don't interfere!' cried Mary. 'You expect me to live this awful life, like a poor white in this terrible house! You're too mean to put ceilings in to make the house a little more comfortable!'

'I told you what to expect when you married me. You can't accuse me of lying to you. And the ceilings . . . you can forget them! I've lived here for six years without ceilings and it hasn't hurt me!' Dick stopped shouting as he began to regret his anger. 'The boy will stay now. Be fair to him and don't make a fool of yourself again.'

Mary walked straight to the kitchen, gave the boy the money he was owed, and told him to leave the house and not return.

'It's not me you're hurting, but yourself,' said Dick. 'Soon you won't be able to get any servants. They'll all know about you and they won't come.'

For a while she did the work herself. She cooked and cleaned, and often cried. This awful life, this unhappiness between the two of them. Deep inside she was building up a great anger and hatred, not only against the native who had left, but against all natives.

She and Dick were invited to a party at the Slatters', but Mary refused to go. She apologised in a very formal note which offended Mrs Slatter. Mrs Slatter felt sorry for Dick for having such a wife, and when Charlie went to see Dick he avoided going to the house.

'Why don't you plant tobacco? You can make money easily,' he suggested, sympathetic to Dick's difficult financial position. But Dick would not listen. 'You're a fool!' said Charlie. 'Don't come to me when your wife is going to have a child and you need money.'

'I've never asked you for anything,' Dick replied angrily, but when Charlie went away he was so worried he felt sick. Perhaps having children would make the situation better. He made himself work harder, but matters in the house did not improve. Mary just could not live in peace with the native servants. A cook never stayed longer than a month, and all the time she was bad-tempered. Sometimes he felt it was all his fault, because life was so hard. But at other times he ran out of the house in anger. If only she could have something to fill her time – that was the main problem.

Chapter 5   The Beginning of the End

Once a month, Dick and Mary took the car to the shop, seven miles away, to buy sacks of flour and other food too heavy to be carried on foot by the servants. Mary had given her order, seen the things put in the car, and was waiting for Dick. As he came out, a man she did not know stopped him and said, 'Well, Jonah,★ another bad year, I suppose?' It was impossible to miss the disrespect in his voice.

She turned to look at the man. Dick smiled. 'I've had good rains this year. Things are not too bad.' Then he got into the car, the smile gone from his face.

★ *Jonah*: the person in the Bible who was punished by God with bad luck and a series of accidents.

'Who was that?' Mary asked.

'I borrowed two hundred pounds from him three years ago, just after we were married.'

'You didn't tell me.'

'I didn't want to worry you. I've paid it back . . . well, except for fifty pounds.'

'Next year, I suppose?'

'With a bit of luck.'

On the drive home, she thought about the way the stranger had spoken to Dick. She was surprised. Of course *she* had no respect for Dick as a husband, as a man, but that did not matter . . . not to her anyway. But she had always felt he was a good farmer, a hardworking man who would in the end succeed with his farm. And then they would have an easier life, just like the other farmers in the area. Now, however, she began to have doubts.

At the shop she had picked up a small book on keeping bees. When they arrived home, she threw it down on the table and went to unpack the shopping. Dick sat at the table and turned the pages of the book. As he read he became more and more interested, and after an hour or so he said to Mary, 'What do you think about keeping bees?'

Mary was not too keen on the idea; it would cost them a lot at the beginning, and it was not certain to make money. But Dick seemed to think they could make at least two hundred pounds a year. 'I'm going to see Charlie Slatter,' he said. 'His brother used to keep bees. I'll ask him what he thinks.' Charlie Slatter advised him not to waste his money, but Dick decided to go ahead anyway. He really believed that by his own hard work he could succeed where others had failed.

For a month he could think of nothing else. He built twenty beehives himself and planted a field with special grass to tempt the bees towards them. He took some of the workers away from their usual jobs and sent them looking for bees every evening. When they were unable to find any, though, he began to lose interest, and Mary was amazed and angry to think of all the time and money that had been wasted. But she was glad to see him return to his normal farm work, paying attention to the crops he knew about.

About six months later the whole thing happened again. 'Mary, I'm going to buy some pigs,' he told her one morning. He refused to listen to her protests, and bought six expensive pigs from Charlie Slatter. The food for the animals was expensive but he was sure it was worth it. After a time the pigs gave birth, and the young pigs died almost immediately of disease.

Mary wanted to scream at Dick for his foolishness, but she tried to keep her anger inside. She began to develop deep lines on her face, and her lips grew thin and tight. She was becoming bitter and hard, and any remaining respect she had for Dick's judgement as a farmer was rapidly disappearing.

After the pigs, he talked of trying other animals; he was sure he could make money from turkeys . . . or perhaps rabbits. At this point, Mary could control herself no longer. She screamed at him, crying until she was too weak to continue, and then she stopped.

Dick looked at her for a long time as she sat there in silence. 'As you like,' he said at last. Mary did not like the way he said this, and she regretted screaming, for she knew that it was a condition of the existence of their marriage that she should pity him generously rather than show open disgust or even disrespect. But there was no more talk of turkeys or rabbits, and for a while it seemed that life had returned to normal.

Then one day he told her that he was going to open a shop on the farm. 'I have a hundred natives here, and there are others who pass through; they'll all buy from our shop.'

He could not have known Mary's feelings about these shops, how they reminded her of the unhappiness of village life as a child. He built one close to the house, and filled it with things that he thought the natives would want. Just before it was ready to be opened, he bought twenty cheap bicycles. All Mary could think about was how the money spent on the shop and all the other money-making ideas could have made her life more comfortable: a bigger house; the ceilings that meant so much to her. When he asked her to work in the shop she could hardly believe it. 'Never,' she replied. 'I would rather die. Selling things to dirty natives!' But in the end she agreed. What else could she do?

She disliked the native men but she hated the women, with their soft brown bodies and their questioning faces. She could see a group of them outside the shop now, waiting for it to open. She hated the way they sat there in the grass with their breasts hanging down for everyone to see, looking as if they did not care whether the shop opened today or tomorrow. But what really made Mary angry was that they always looked so satisfied and calm.

She could delay the opening no longer. Going outside, she looked towards the group of women, then walked slowly towards the shop. The women crowded in, touching everything, speaking loudly in languages Mary did not understand. The women were everywhere, their children hanging on their backs, or holding their skirts. These little ones looked in amazement at her white skin from eyes half-covered with flies. She stood in the shop for half an hour, but suddenly could not stay there any longer. 'Hurry up now!' she shouted coldly. The talking and laughing stopped as they felt her dislike for them. One by one they went away.

It was the shop that finished Mary. The bicycles were never sold and although each month they lost more and more money, Dick would not close it. As time went by she started to think of the town again. She persuaded herself that if only she could go back there her life would be good . . . everything could be the way it was before.

One day she noticed an advertisement in the paper. Her old job was free! The following morning, after Dick had left for the fields, she packed her suitcase and started walking to the Slatters' farm.

She could delay opening the shop no longer. The women crowded in, touching everything, speaking loudly in languages Mary did not understand.

'Where's Dick?' said Charlie Slatter when she asked him to drive her to the station.

'He's . . . he's working. He's busy.' He gave her a strange look, but drove her where she wanted to go. She did not like Charlie Slatter; nor did she suspect that he wanted Dick's farm to fail so that he could buy the land cheaply for himself.

When she arrived in town she went straight to the club. Her heart lifted as the building came into view. It was such a lovely day; the sun was shining and there was a cool, light wind. Everything seemed different, even the sky. The streets and houses looked fresh and clean, not at all like the farm. It was a different world! It was her world!

The trouble started at the club. No, she could not stay there — it was not for married women. Strange, she had never really thought of herself as being married. She booked into a cheap hotel.

At her old office, none of the girls working there knew her. When she was shown into her old employer's room, his face made her look down at her clothes. She was wearing an old dress — not at all fashionable — and her shoes were covered with red dust. 'I'm sorry, Mary,' he said. 'The job has already been filled.' There was a long moment of silence. 'Have you been ill?' he asked.

'No,' she replied sadly.

Back in her hotel room she stared at herself in the mirror. 'I'll go and buy a new dress. And I'll have my hair done,' she thought. But then she remembered that she had no money. How would she pay for her hotel room? She sat down on a chair and remained still, wondering what to do. She appeared to be waiting for something. When there was a knock on the door, she looked as if she had been expecting it, and Dick's entrance did not change her face.

'Mary, don't leave me,' he said quietly.

She stood up, tidied her hair and stood before him. There was to be no anger, no discussion. Seeing her like this, Dick said she could go and buy herself some new clothes.

'What shall I use for money?' she asked.

They were back together again, and nothing had changed. Life on the farm was even worse than before. She no longer had her daydreams of the town to keep her going. She knew now that there was nothing there for her. This was the beginning of the end for Mary. She could no longer feel. She could no longer fight.

Like her mother, who had simply died of unhappiness after a short illness, Mary no longer wished to live. She could not stay, and she could not run away. But there was a sudden and unexpected change in her life which kept her going for a little while. A few months after her return, and six years after she had married him, Dick got ill for the first time.

Chapter 6   Mary Takes Responsibility

Winter came, and seemed to breathe new life into Mary. The days were cool and the evenings quite cold. One day she went with Dick to the fields to see the unfamiliar frost lying thinly on the earth. She picked up small pieces and held them between her fingers, inviting him to do the same. They were closer together these days than they had ever been before.

But it was then that Dick became ill and the new feeling between them, which might have grown, was not yet strong enough to live through this fresh trouble. He was hit suddenly by malaria and, because he had never been ill before, took it badly and became difficult. He lay in his bed for days, from time to time asking Mary about the farm, for he knew that nothing would get done if he was not there to watch the natives. She realised that he wanted her to go down and see to things, but did not like to suggest it. In the end, though, she felt she had to go, or Dick would try to get up before he was well.

She hated the idea of mixing with the natives in the fields. As she left the house with the car keys in her hand she noticed the whip hanging near the door and took it down. She turned it around in her fingers; it made her feel strong.

When she arrived at the fields, there were no natives to be seen. They knew of Dick's illness, of course, and had returned to their huts. She walked to the place where they lived on the edge of the farm. How she disliked coming here: flies everywhere, naked children, women with their breasts showing.

Looking through doors she could see men asleep; other men stood and watched her.

She found the head boy and spoke to him angrily: 'Get the boys out into the fields! I'll take money off the wages of everyone who is not at work in ten minutes.'

None of the men moved, and there was laughter from some of the women sitting near. 'Ten minutes,' she said sharply, then turned and walked away.

The first of the workers reached the fields half an hour later, and by the end of an hour no more than half the men were there. She called the head boy and took the names of those who were still missing, then she sat in the car and watched. There was almost no talking; the natives hated a woman being there, watching them. At lunch-time she returned to the house but did not tell tell Dick exactly what had happened, because she did not want to worry him. In the afternoon she drove down again. She was beginning to like this strange new feeling of responsibility for the farm.

This time she left the car and walked in the fields among the workers. In her hand was the whip. It made her feel powerful against the hatred of the natives. Whenever one of the boys stopped working she looked at her watch, and as soon as one minute had passed she shouted at him to get on. All afternoon she did this. How could she know that it was Dick's habit to give them a five-minute rest every hour?

At the end of the week the workers came to the house to be paid. They made a queue in front of the table at which Mary was sitting. One by one she paid them, carefully counting out the money from a box. As she came to those who had not been at work at all on that first day, she took off ten per cent of their wages. There was anger among the natives, which grew from low whispers to angry shouts.

'Tell them that if they don't like it they can get off the farm,' she told the head boy firmly, picking up the table and going back into the house. The protests continued but at last the natives went away.

She was filled with a feeling of victory. 'Dirty kaffirs!' she said to Dick. 'How they smell!'

'They think we smell bad too, you know,' replied Dick. 'What was all the noise about?'

'Oh, nothing much.' She had decided not to tell him that some of the boys were leaving, at least until he was well.

'I hope you're being careful with them. It's not easy to get workers these days.'

'I don't believe in being soft with them. If I had my way, I'd use this whip on all of them. They make me sick!'

She was beginning to find out more and more about how the farm worked. She looked at all the crops and spent a long time analysing Dick's cash books. At first she thought she must be mistaken, but she soon realised that the farm was a disaster, and could see easily the causes of their poverty. She realised bitterly that her husband was a complete fool. There was not a single thing done properly on the whole place. He was growing the wrong crops. He started things that he never finished. How could he not see his mistakes?

Dick was getting better now, and on the last day before he returned to work, Mary was in the fields as usual. She watched the natives, thinking about the changes that needed to be made to the farm. Suddenly she noticed that one of the boys was not working. He had fallen out of line and seemed to be breathing heavily. She looked at her watch. One minute passed, then two. She waited until three minutes had gone before shouting, 'Get back to work.' The native looked at her slowly, then turned away. He was going to fetch some water from the petrol tin that stood in the shadows under a tree. She spoke again, sharply, her voice rising: 'I said get back to work!'

He turned to face her. 'I want a drink,' he said in a language she did not understand.

30

'Don't speak to me in that language,' she screamed. She looked around for the head boy, but he was not in sight.

The man said in English, very slowly, 'I . . . want . . . water,' and suddenly smiled and pointed to his mouth.

The other natives, who had stopped working, started to laugh. She thought they were laughing at her, and was so angry that she could hardly speak.

'Don't speak English to me!' she shouted at last, and then stopped.

The man looked around at the others as if to say, 'She won't let me speak my own language and now I mustn't speak English. What other language is there?'

She opened her mouth again, but nothing came out as she saw open amusement in the eyes of the native.

Without thinking, she raised the whip high and brought it down hard across his face. Blood burst from his cheek as she looked, and a drop ran down his chin and fell on to his chest. He was a huge man, bigger than all the others, wearing only a small piece of cloth around his waist. She stood still, terrified at what would happen next. She knew all the natives were standing around her. 'Now get back to work,' she shouted. For a moment the man looked at her in a way that made her stomach turn liquid with fear. Then slowly he went away and they all began to work silently. She was shaking with fear at what she had done and at the look she had seen in the man's eyes.

She had planned to have a long argument with Dick that night, now that he was well again. It had seemed so easy when she was down in the fields, but when he was in front of her she found it difficult to begin to tell him how he should reorganise the farm. He was busy preparing himself for the next day but did not discuss the farm with her, and she felt insulted. Had she not had full responsibility for it during the last few weeks?

Two days later, when Dick seemed fully himself again, she

31

began. She painted a picture for him of exactly how the farm was operating, and what money he could expect in return if there were no crop failures or bad seasons. She showed him quite clearly that they would never escape from poverty if they continued as they had been. She spoke for some time, showing him the figures she had written on a piece of paper, and while she talked he felt both admiration and self-pity. Although she was making some mistakes over detail, in general she was right; every cruel thing she said was true! But he felt hurt that she did not seem to understand – for him the farm was not just a money-making machine; he loved the earth and planted trees to put something back into the land, not to get rich! She told him they should grow tobacco, not small food crops; tobacco would make money.

'And when we've made money? What then?' said Dick slowly.

She looked at him. She had not really thought of the future very clearly. She dreamed of getting out of this awful poverty trap. When she thought of what she wanted, she could only imagine herself back in town at the club, leading her own life. Dick did not fit into this picture. So when he repeated his question, she looked away and replied quickly, 'Well, we can't go on like this, can we?'

Then he knew. He realised that she saw a future in the town – a place where he could never live. He loved every tree on his land and he knew he could never live anywhere else. Should he work towards a future which would lead to Mary leaving the farm . . . and leaving him? But perhaps when things got better – and when they had children – she would see how good life could be. But he was afraid, and he did not know what to do next.

At last he looked up and with an unhappy, twisted smile said, 'Well, can I think about it for a few days?'

'I'm going to bed,' she replied sharply, and left him sitting there alone with his thoughts.

Three days later he told her quietly that he had arranged for two new buildings to be put up. When he looked towards her, he saw that her eyes were full of a new hope. But she could not hide the feeling of victory over him.

Chapter 7 Moses

Now Mary left Dick to get on with the work on the farm. She did not interfere and both of them knew how important it was that Dick should succeed with the tobacco crop.

She watched with excitement as the new buildings went up, and could hardly wait for the rains to come to see the young tobacco plants growing in the fields. The rains came on time that year and for almost a month the crop grew steadily. But soon after Christmas the rain stopped. No more rain fell for weeks; the ground became dry and the plants began to die. The rains did come again, but it was too late. When Dick told Mary what had happened she felt he was glad. But she could not blame him, because it was clearly not his fault. When he explained that they would have to borrow more money to keep the farm going, Mary begged him to try tobacco again for just one more year . . . to plant even more land and risk everything on the rains being good next year.

'We can't have bad rains for two years,' she said with desperation in her voice.

'But if we do, we'll lose the farm,' replied Dick.

'If we do, we do. Maybe that would be a good thing,' she shouted.

But Dick would not agree to rely on a tobacco crop again and Mary gave up trying to persuade him. He was pleasantly surprised that she did not seem to be too unhappy . . . at least, she was not showing obvious signs of it at the moment. So Dick prepared once again to face the coming year on the farm, hoping that things would improve.

For Mary, the tobacco crop had been her last hope, and its failure had a powerful effect on her. Her dreams were gone and she began to lose all interest in things around her. She was tired. Her days were spent in the house where she did little, but found it difficult to sit still. Her nights were restless and she slept badly. She did what she had to do in a mechanical way. After a while even these movements slowed to a complete stop and she spent her days sitting quietly on the sofa. She felt that she had somehow gone over the edge and could not return.

'I want to have a child,' she said one day.

Now for years Dick had wanted children, but he had always felt they were too poor. Mary had never encouraged his wish for a family.

'But the money, Mary. We haven't got the money. School bills, books, train fares, clothes . . . we just can't afford it at the moment.'

Then they argued. But they both knew it was a foolish idea to have a child now, and the subject was never mentioned again.

Time passed, and Mary came to see the sad truth about their lives more clearly. Dick was kind to her but she had no respect for him. There was no hope for their future. They could only continue to be miserable; they would always be poor whites. And now she gave way completely. All day she sat on the sofa with her eyes shut, feeling the heat beating down. For weeks she spoke to no one but Dick and the servant, and Dick saw her only for five minutes in the morning and for half an hour before he fell into bed exhausted at the end of the day. Then, in the full heat of the summer, the latest servant told her he was leaving.

By now Mary had a name among the natives for being a terrible employer, and Dick found it impossible to get a new servant. He decided to bring one of the farm workers up to the house. Mary could teach him what to do.

When the native came, Mary immediately recognised him as the one she had hit with the whip that day in the fields. 'He's the best one I can find,' said Dick; he knew nothing about this earlier event. Mary said nothing, and the boy, Moses, stayed.

She began teaching him what to do in the house, but she was not able to behave towards him in the way she had with the others. She could not forget that day and in the back of her mind she feared that he would attack her. But he acted like the rest. He was silent and patient and kept his eyes down at all times. She used to sit watching him. The white shirt and shorts she had given him were too small; his strong arms filled out the thin cloth of the sleeves until she thought it would burst. He was a good worker, and he showed no sign of remembering that she had hit him. She soon became used to him and began to shout at him in her normal way. But things were not quite the same as before.

She tried not to be around when the boy had his daily wash. One morning, though, after she had collected eggs from the chicken houses, she found herself standing a few yards from him. He had his back to her and was washing his neck. As she looked he turned, by some chance, and saw her. He stood up straight and waited for her to leave. She was filled with anger and embarrassment at the idea that this native should think she was there on purpose and felt that she wanted to hit him, just as she had done before. But she turned away and walked back to the house. This was the first time she had felt anything at all for months: the sharp stones under her feet; the heat of the sun on her neck; his eyes on her back.

In the house, she was as nervous as if she had put her hand on a dangerous snake. She moved between the kitchen and the sitting room, thinking of that thick, black, powerful neck. The way he had looked seemed to threaten the normal ways of behaving between black and white, between servant and employer. She felt a deep anger and had to do something at once. When he returned to the house, she shouted at him: 'Wash this floor!'

'I washed it this morning,' said the native slowly, his eyes burning into her.

She tried not to be around when the boy had his daily wash.
One morning though, she found herself standing a few yards
from him.

'I said, wash it. Do it at once!' Her voice rose on these last words. For a moment they looked at each other with hatred.

She lay down on the sofa as he washed the floor. She was shaking. She could feel the blood in her ears, and her mouth was dry. When he had finished, she said sharply, 'It's time to lay the table.' She watched him closely. Every movement he made angered her but every time she gave him an order, he followed her instructions patiently and well. When he spoke to her, he spoke politely. Later he stood silently outside the back door in the sun, looking at nothing, not moving. She wanted to scream, but there was nothing more for him to do. Again she moved around the house, the anger still boiling inside her. Then she went into the bedroom and burst into tears, trying to hide the sound of her crying from the native. She cried for some time; then, as she lifted her eyes to dry them, saw the clock. Dick would be home soon and he must not see her like this. She washed her face, combed her hair, and put some powder on the dark bags under her eyes.

That meal was silent as all their meals were. He looked at her face and knew what was wrong. It was always because of rows with the servants that she cried. But he was disappointed, for he thought she had stopped having arguments with them. She ate nothing, keeping her head bent down as Moses moved quietly around the table.

When the native was out of the room, Dick said angrily, 'Mary, you must keep this boy. He's the best we have ever had. No more changing servants; I've had enough. I'm warning you, Mary.'

She did not reply; she was weak with the tears and anger of the morning. He looked at her in surprise; he had expected her to shout back at him as she usually did. Her silence made him continue. 'Mary,' he said, 'did you hear what I said?'

'Yes,' she answered with difficulty.

When Dick left, she went immediately to the bedroom to avoid the sight of the native clearing the table. She slept all afternoon waiting for her husband's return.

Chapter 8　Illness and Desire

And so the days passed, through August and September; hot days with slow winds that picked up dust from the fields and carried it everywhere. The knowledge that the native was in the house with her all day lay like a weight at the back of her mind. She kept him working as long as she could, then she sat silently for hours on the sofa. She felt that the house was a place of battle between two forces – Moses and herself. But she could not fight properly because of Dick's warning that he would not allow any more changes of servants. Most of the time her mind seemed completely empty. Sometimes she tried to speak, but she started a sentence and forgot to finish it. Dick could see that she was slipping further and further away from him.

With Moses, though, her mind was sharp. She thought of all the things she would say and do to him, and then she thought that she could not for fear that he would leave and make Dick angry again. One day she found she was talking to herself – saying the words she wanted to shout at Moses, punishing him for not cleaning a room well with cruel words that he would not understand in English. Then she stopped, terrified that Moses had heard her. Opening the back door, she saw him resting, as usual, against the wall of the house; standing without moving in the heat of the sun, eyes looking straight ahead at nothing. She avoided him all that day, went to her bedroom and cried hopelessly.

The next day Moses told her he was going to leave at the end of the month. She wanted to shout at him . . . she wanted him to go. She opened her mouth to speak, but stopped suddenly, thinking of Dick's anger. To her horror, she found she was beginning to cry again – in front of the native! For some time neither of them moved, though she continued to cry.

'You mustn't go,' she begged, filled with shame at her own words. 'Please, you must stay.'

He fetched a glass of water, came to her and said simply, 'Drink!' She did not move, so he lifted the glass to her lips and she drank. Then she stood there, unable to leave. What was happening? 'Now missus lie down on the bed.' He put out his hand and pushed her by the shoulder towards the bedroom. It was like a bad dream. She had never in her life touched a native. As she got nearer to the bed, she felt her head begin to swim and her bones go soft. 'Missus lie down,' he said. And this time his voice was gentle, almost like a father. He took her coat off the back of the door and lay it across her feet, then left the room. She lay there silently, unable to think about what had happened, and what the effect of this might be on the future. She stayed in her room all that day until Dick came back. He saw she had been crying, but neither of them mentioned it.

A week passed, and she began to realise that Moses was not going. She tried to forget that she had begged him to stay, for the shame was too much. But one day he turned to her in the kitchen, and said in a hard voice, 'Missus asked me to stay. I stay to help missus. If missus angry again, I go.' She did not know what to say; she felt helpless. What was happening? How could a native speak to a white woman like this? But she said nothing.

When the rains started in October, Dick stayed in the fields all day. He did not return for lunch because there was so much work to do. Mary told Moses she would not take lunch while Dick was away. But on the first day that Dick was away at lunch-time, Moses brought her a meal of eggs, jam and toast.

'I told you I didn't want anything,' she said to him sharply.

'Missus ate no breakfast. She must eat,' he replied quietly. And she began to eat.

Things were different between them now. The power she had felt over him as his employer had gone. She was helpless before him. Her feelings were confused. She knew she was afraid of him, but she could not admit to herself that she also found him attractive. She never checked on his work now, and he did what he liked in the house. Once, when Dick was late home from the fields, she decided to go and look for him. 'No, I go,' said Moses, and she let him. These days she often watched Moses going about his work – not in the way an employer watches a servant, but with a fearful curiosity. Every day he looked after her, bringing her presents of eggs, or flowers that he had picked near the house.

Dick fell ill again with malaria, and for the first two nights of the illness Mary sat up with him. During the day, she drove out to the fields. As she expected, the boys had stopped work, but this time she did nothing. She did not care any more; she had lost all interest in the farm. Back at the house she sat in silence, exhausted and empty.

On the third morning of Dick's illness, Moses asked, 'Did missus go to bed last night?' and she answered, 'No.' Dick became much worse that day, and by the evening his temperature had risen to 105. In the early hours of the morning Moses came to the bedroom door. 'Missus stay in the other room tonight. I stay here.'

'No, I must stay with him.'

But he insisted, and after a while she left. 'You call me if he wakes up,' she said, trying to remind him that she was his employer.

She went over to the sofa. She hated the idea of spending a whole night with only a brick wall separating her from the black man next door. She lay down and put a coat over her feet. It was a restless sleep, full of strange, horrible dreams.

She was a child again, playing in the small dusty garden in front of the small wood and metal house, with friends who, in her dreams, had no faces. She heard her mother's sharp call and went into the house, but could not find her anywhere. At the bedroom door she stopped, feeling sick. There was her father, the little man with the fat stomach whom she hated, holding her mother in his arms as they stood by the window. Her mother was laughing. As her father bent over his wife, Mary ran away.

Again she was playing. This time her father caught her head and held it against the top of his legs with his small hairy hands to cover her eyes, laughing and joking about her mother hiding. She could smell the unwashed maleness that her father always smelt of. She tried to get away but he held her down until she could hardly breathe. Screaming in her sleep, she half woke.

Thinking she must be awake, she listened for sounds from the next room. There was nothing. In her dream she believed Dick was dead, and that the black man was waiting next door to kill her too. She got up from the sofa and walked slowly to the bedroom. All she could see was the shape of Dick lying under the blankets. She could not see the black man, but she knew he was there waiting in the shadows. She opened the curtain a little and now she could see him. He was asleep against the wall, but woke now and sat up slowly. She looked across at the bed again where Dick lay still. He looked ugly; his face was yellow. He was dead. She felt guilty at the wave of gladness that came over her, and tried to feel sorry as she knew she should.

The native was watching her carefully. He was standing now, moving slowly and powerfully towards her, and it was not only he, but also her father, who approached. She could smell her father's smell again. She was afraid . . . so afraid. Her legs were liquid with fear and she was beginning to have difficulty in breathing. She rested against the wall and almost fell through the half-open window. He came near and put his hand gently on her arm. It was the voice of the African she heard, but at the same time it was her father, frightening and horrible, who touched her with desire.

She screamed, knowing suddenly that she was dreaming. She screamed desperately, trying to wake herself up. The noise must be waking Dick. Then she was awake and Moses was standing at her side holding a cup of tea. Seeing him, she pulled herself back into the corner of the sofa, watching him with terror in her eyes, trying to separate what was real from her dreams.

'He sleep,' Moses said. But still she watched the black man

carefully, unable to speak. He gave her a curious look, surprised at her fear; he seemed to be judging her.

'Why is missus afraid of me?' he asked.

'Don't be stupid; I'm not afraid of you,' she said in a high voice, shaking a little. It was the voice of a woman speaking to a white man whom she finds attractive. As she heard the words come out of her mouth, and saw the effect on the man's face, she was horrified. He gave her a long, slow look; then he left the room.

When he had gone, she forced herself to stand and walk around. Dick was sleeping in the bedroom. It was still dark outside. She went to sit with Dick and stayed there all that day. And that night she locked all the doors of the house and went to bed beside Dick – thankful, perhaps for the first time in their marriage, for his closeness.

Within a week, Dick was back at work. Again the days passed, the long days alone in the house with the African while Dick was out in the fields. She was fighting against something she could not understand. Moses filled her thoughts night and day, while Dick became less and less real. She could never be calm; the native was always there. She kept out of his way as much as possible, and she could not look into his eyes. She knew that it would mean disaster if she did, because now there was always the memory of her fear, of the way she had spoken to him that night. She hated hearing him speak because now his voice sounded different: confident, powerful, almost rude. She wanted to tell Dick to send him away but she did not dare.

She felt she was in a street, moving towards something final, something she could not see but from which there was no escape. She felt she was waiting, and Moses seemed to be waiting too. They were like two fighters silently preparing for a battle. But while he was strong, she was frightened and weak from her terrible dream-filled nights.

Chapter 9   Six Months Away

All these years Dick and Mary had never taken any part in the life of the other white farmers in the district. They had no idea that these other families talked about them endlessly. How could they know, for they never saw anybody? But people calling on the Slatters always asked about the Turners and Mrs Slatter, who had long ago given up trying to be pleasant to Mary, did not hesitate to tell them about the strange things that had happened on the Turners' farm; how they lived like pigs, how Mary had tried to run away but Dick had brought her back. As the stories became exaggerated, the belief grew that Dick was a terrible husband who regularly beat his wife. Charlie felt only disgust for Mary and did not like these stories about Dick. For although he had no respect for Dick as a farmer, he liked him and felt that most of his problems were caused by being married to that awful woman. So he spoke his mind and gradually people started to believe him.

The real reason why Charlie had an interest in the Turners, though, was that he wanted their farm. For years Charlie had taken from his own land and put nothing back. The earth had been rich and had produced good crops, but now it produced little. This did not really matter to the Slatters, since they had plenty of money, but their animals needed grass to eat. Charlie looked with envy at the dark earth of Dick's farm, for Dick had over the years planted trees and crops that kept it rich; he had always looked after it well. For years Charlie had been waiting for Dick to give up and sell the farm, but through all the bad seasons and crop failures, Dick had continued in his own stubborn way.

One day Charlie realised, with some guilt, that he had not visited Dick for nearly two years, and that afternoon he drove to the Turners' farm. As he went, he looked carefully at the crops and buildings. Nothing was any different; things looked neither better nor worse than before.

'What can I do for you?' said Dick as Charlie stopped his car in the field where he was working.

'Nothing. Just came to see how you were doing.'

They sat for a while watching the natives, until Dick stood up with difficulty. 'End of another day.'

Charlie looked at him carefully. 'Are you sick? You don't look well.'

'Oh, I'm all right. Blood's getting thin after all these years, that's all.'

But Charlie could see he was ill. In fact Dick was often ill these days. He had by now suffered several times from malaria.

'How's Mary?' asked Charlie, and Dick told him that he was very worried about her. He invited Charlie up to the house. Since Dick had sold his car because he could no longer afford to keep it, they climbed into Charlie's.

'But what's wrong with her, man?' Charlie asked.

Dick was quiet for a moment. 'I don't know,' he said at last. 'She's just different. Sometimes I think she's better, and then things start getting worse again. She's just not the same as she was before. You know . . . she used to keep chickens, made a lot out of them every month. Now she's let it go. And she used to drive me mad with her complaining about the servants. Now she just says nothing.'

Charlie looked at him. 'Look here, Turner,' he said suddenly. 'Why don't you give up the farm? You're not doing yourself or your wife any good.'

'Oh, we keep going,' said Dick.

'But you're ill.'

'I'm all right.'

Charlie stopped the car in front of the house. 'Why don't you sell to me? I'll give you a good price.'

'Where would I go?' asked Dick in amazement. 'No, we'll be all right.'

'Evening, Mrs Turner,' said Charlie, as they entered the house.

'Good evening,' said Mary. She was wearing a red cotton dress and long brightly coloured earrings of the kind the natives liked so much. She looked thin and uncertain, but her blue eyes seemed to have a new light in them. 'Why, good evening, Mr Slatter,' she said girlishly. 'We haven't seen you for a long time!' She laughed strangely, and Dick looked away, suffering. He hated it when she was like this.

She seemed to Charlie a little mad. He sat down and looked around the room. The curtains were torn, a window was broken. Everywhere were bits and pieces of cloth that they had been unable to sell in the shop. 'We closed the shop,' said Dick, 'so we're using the stuff ourselves.'

'Moses, Moses!' Mary called. Nothing happened. 'Excuse me, you know what these boys are,' she said, and went to the kitchen.

Charlie looked at Dick as if asking him to explain, but Dick looked away again. Supper, when it was brought in, was tea, bread and butter, and a piece of cold meat. The plates were cracked and the knives were dirty. Charlie could hardly bring himself to eat. Through the meal Mary continued to talk in sharp bursts about this and that, and kept bending her head in a way which shook her earrings while smiling at Charlie. He was disgusted at the way she was acting, and answered her questions coldly and in as few words as possible.

'Would you like some fruit, Mr Slatter? Moses, fetch the oranges.'

Charlie looked up in surprise at the voice she had used to speak to the native. She was speaking to him in that same girlish manner.

'Oranges finished,' Moses replied rudely.

'No, there are some. I know there are.'

'Oranges finished,' said Moses louder, looking her in the eye.

Charlie was amazed. The power in the native's voice was obvious to anybody. He looked at Mary. Her face showed fear.

'How long have you had this boy?' he asked sharply. Moses was standing at the door, openly listening.

'About four years,' said Dick quietly.

'Why do you let him speak to you like that?'

Neither of them replied. Mary was looking over her shoulder to where Moses stood. The look in her face caused Charlie to shout suddenly, 'Get out! Get on with your work!' Moses disappeared. Charlie waited for Dick to speak, but his head was bent and he said nothing.

'Get rid of that boy, Turner. Get rid of him!' Charlie ordered.

He took Dick outside the house. 'Listen, Turner, you've got to get away from here. I'll buy your farm and you can stay on as manager. But you must go away for six months first. You have to take a holiday. Take your wife away from here.' He spoke quickly, giving Dick no chance to refuse. He was obeying a law of the whites in Southern Africa: 'You must not let any whites sink below a certain point, because if you do the niggers will think they are just as good.' Poor Dick, though, felt that Charlie was asking him to give up everything he had . . . even his life itself. 'You must go away. I'll get someone to look after the place for six months. Then you come back as manager.' For four hours they talked, until at last Dick gave in.

As soon as Charlie left, Mary returned to her old ways. She no longer spoke to Dick at all. It was as if he did not exist for her. She came alive only when Moses entered the room, and then she never took her eyes off him. Dick did not know what this meant; he did not want to know, because he was beyond fighting now.

Charlie Slatter wasted no time. He soon found a young man just out from England to manage the farm while Dick was away, and Tony Marston moved into a small one-roomed building at the back of the house. The walls were mud and the floor was the bare earth, but Tony did not mind these things. He was excited at being in Africa. It was so much better than the office job he had left in

England. At twenty he was ready for some adventure. He wanted to learn to farm, and working here would be good experience. He was sorry for Dick, but even this tragedy seemed to him romantic. He was expected to pick up enough knowledge in one month with Dick to keep the farm going for six months, so he worked hard and spent every day in the fields.

For Dick that month was hard. Fifteen years of his life were about to disappear. The earth that he loved, the trees and the crops that were in his blood – all these would be gone for ever.

Mary too showed no pleasure at the thought of going on her first holiday for years. She was making no preparations. In fact neither she nor Dick ever mentioned it. Tony hardly saw her, but the few words she did speak to him seemed to make no sense. He thought she was probably slightly mad.

Three days before they were to leave the farm, Tony asked to stay behind for the afternoon because he was not feeling well. He awoke from sleep at about four in the afternoon, feeling very thirsty. He walked towards the house and opened the door quietly because he had been told that Mary slept in the afternoons. He filled his glass and turned to leave. As he did so he could see into the bedroom, and what he saw made him stop suddenly. Mary was sitting on the bed in her underwear, and Moses stood behind her, helping her to pull her dress back on again. When she was dressed she said, 'Thank you, Moses. You'd better go now. It's time for my husband to come.' The native turned to leave and noticed Tony. He stopped and gave him a long, evil look that made Tony quite afraid. Then he walked past. Tony stood still for a moment, wondering what to do next.

Mary too came out of the bedroom. When she saw Tony, she looked at him with sudden fear. Then the fear seemed to disappear and her face looked empty.

'Does that native always dress you?' he asked.

'He has so little to do. He must earn his money.' There was

silence for a moment. 'They said I was not like that, not like that, not like that!' she sang.

'This woman really is crazy,' thought Tony.

'It's been so long . . . I should have got out years ago . . . But I can't . . . He won't go away . . .!' she shouted.

Now he wanted to help her, but Moses appeared at the door. 'Go away,' ordered Tony. 'Go away at once!'

'Yes, go away,' Mary shouted at Moses. Tony realised she was using him to try and get back some of the power that she had lost.

'Missus want me to go?' the boy asked quietly.

'Get out!' shouted Tony again. 'Get out before I kick you out!'

After a long, slow, look of hatred, the native went. And then he was gone. There was an uncomfortable silence.

'You sent him away!' she screamed at Tony. 'He'll never come back! He's gone! He's gone! Everything was all right until you came!' And she fell to the floor in tears.

What should he say to Turner? He decided to advise him to get rid of the native. But Moses did not return. When Dick asked where he was, Mary said that she had sent him away. Tony heard the emptiness in her voice and saw that she was speaking to Dick without seeing him. He decided to do nothing. What more could he do? The next morning he went off to the fields with Dick as usual. It was their last day together, and there was a lot to do.

Chapter 10   The Last Day

Mary woke suddenly. It was a still night, and Dick lay asleep beside her. Today her mind was clear and her body was comfortable. For a while she stayed without moving. Then she began to cry.

Dick turned to her in his half-sleep. 'What's wrong, Mary?' he whispered.

'Go to sleep, Dick,' she said. 'It's not morning yet.' And he was soon asleep again.

She sat up straight, feeling bitter. He was always there; he never left her in peace. She felt pulled in two different directions, and she tried to go back to that part of her mind where Dick did not exist. It had been a choice, between Dick and the other, and Dick had been destroyed long ago. 'Poor Dick,' she said to herself, and then she did not think of him again.

She got out of bed and stood by the window. The stars were gone, and the sky was colourless and huge. A pink glow spread slowly across the sky and the dark trees rose to meet it. The beauty of the scene filled her with a calm that she had not felt for years. But the night was nearly over. When the sun rose, her moment would be gone and she would lose for ever this peace that now filled her. Gradually the insects began to make their morning calls and the dull red ball came up over the fields. The world became small, shut in a room of heat and light. She knew he was out there somewhere, resting against a tree, waiting, his eyes fixed on the house. But it would not be yet. No. She knew she had the whole day in front of her.

When Dick and the young man had left for work, she returned to her usual position on the sofa. 'What was it all about?' she wondered dully. 'I don't understand. I don't understand!' She saw herself now as others would see her afterwards – an ugly, pitiful woman. 'How did it come to this? The evil is there, I can feel it . . . I've lived with it for all these years! But what have I done?' What had she done? She felt controlled by things she did not understand, pushed towards the night that she knew would finish her.

She looked around at the house. 'It will be killed and swallowed by the trees when we have gone.' She could see the future clearly. First the rats would come – she could already hear them at night on the roof. And then the insects would follow, and settle in the holes in the brick. The rain would beat down endlessly, grass would grow through the floor and the branches of trees would push through the broken windows.

She could not stay in the house any longer. She ran outside into the trees. 'I'll find *him* and it'll all be over.' Her body was wet with sweat, and the sound of insects shook the earth all around her. She stopped, breathing hard. Lifting her eyes she saw that she was standing in the full sun, a sun that seemed so low she could reach out and touch it. She stretched out her hand, but it brushed against some wet leaves and a huge insect suddenly flew out. With a cry of horror she ran through the long grass back towards the house.

She stopped suddenly. A native was standing there. She put her hand to her mouth . . . but it was not him. The man put a piece of paper in her hand. It said: 'I shall not be back for lunch. Too busy. Send down tea and sandwiches.'

When the native had gone, she thought about Dick again. He had been kind to her. Suddenly she thought that perhaps he could save her. But she looked out over the fields. No. They knew she was going to die.

Hours later she woke up. She had slept through her last day. The young man! He would save her. She left the house and walked towards the small building in which he lived. She went in. Oh it was so cool, so good! She sat on his bed and put her head in her hands. Then she pulled herself up. She must not sleep again. She looked around at the young man's things. And remembered: 'But I haven't been to the shop.' She knew she must go.

She stopped in front of the shop. How she hated it! There it was at her death as it had been all her life. She kicked the door. It opened and she looked into the darkness. And there he stood, Moses, the black man, looking at her in his lazy way. She gave a little cry and ran back out, but he did not follow her.

She returned to the house to wait.

'Have you finished packing, Mary?' asked Dick when he came back. 'You know we have to leave tomorrow.'

'Tomorrow!' she said, laughing. Dick left the room, his hand covering his face.

Later, when Dick asked her to come to bed, she went to lock the back door and came face to face with Moses standing in the darkness. 'He's there!' she said to Dick, her voice a whisper. 'He's outside!'

Dick went outside with a lamp, but he couldn't see anyone.

'Aren't you getting undressed?' said Dick at last in his hopeless, patient voice. She pulled off her clothes and lay awake in bed, looking at the roof.

'Mary, listen to me. You must see a doctor. You're ill.'

'Of course I'm ill. I've been ill ever since I came to this place.'

There was silence and soon Dick was asleep. She listened to the night outside and slowly a terror began to fill her. Her eyes were alive with light, and against the light she saw a dark, waiting shape. She sat up again. He was in the room, just beside her! But the room was empty. There was nothing. A storm started outside. She heard the thunder in the distance and the lightning lit up the room now and then. She was alone. She was shut inside a small black box, and it seemed to her that a huge black spider was moving across the roof, trying to get in. She was trapped. She knew she would have to go out and meet him. Slowly she got up and, full of fear, moved towards the door and stood, looking out.

Then, as she heard the thunder crash and shake the trees, the sky lit up, and she saw a man's shape move from the dark and come towards her. Two yards away, Moses stopped. She could see his great shoulders, the shape of his head, his shining eyes. And at the sight of him her feelings suddenly changed, and she was filled with guilt. But she felt she only had to move forward and explain, and the

*Mary opened her mouth to speak and, as she did so, saw his hand with
something long in it, lifted above his head, and she knew it would be
too late.*

terror would go away. She opened her mouth to speak and, as she
did so, saw his hand with something long in it, lifted above his head,
and she knew it would be too late. All her past slipped away and
when she tried to scream he put his big black hand over her mouth.
The trees rushed towards her like animals, and the thunder was the
noise of their coming. Her last sight of the world as she was pushed
against the wall was of his other hand crashing down towards her
head. She fell forwards across the floor and lay at his feet.

It was beginning to rain. Big drops fell on to Moses' back, and
another dripping sound made him look down at the piece of metal
he held. Blood was falling from it on to the brick floor. He dropped
the weapon suddenly, as if in fear. Then he stopped and picked it up

again. He turned and walked out on to the steps, put the weapon in his belt and washed his hands in the rain. He seemed to be cleaning himself, preparing to deny knowledge of what had just happened. Then he stopped again and looked about him. He pulled out the weapon, looked at it and simply threw it on the floor beside Mary.

Moses turned his back on the house and walked slowly towards the small building where the Englishman lived. He stood at the door, looking into the blackness and listening carefully. There was no sound of breathing. He went towards the bed, and there was his enemy, asleep. He looked at him with hatred for a moment, then left him there and returned to the house.

Standing at the top of the steps, it was too dark to see clearly. He waited for lightning to light up the front of the house and it came. As he looked for one last time on Mary's body, he enjoyed his final moment of revenge, a moment so perfect and complete that it made him forget all thoughts of escape. Then he walked slowly off through the rain into the bush. After a few hundred yards he stopped, thought for a moment, and sat down beside a tree. He was still there when they came to take him away.

ACTIVITIES

Chapters 1–2

Before you read

1 Look at the picture on page 5. The black man in shorts and the large
   white man are looking at each other. What do you think each man is
   thinking about the other at that moment and why?

2 Find these words in your dictionary and check their meanings, if you
   are not sure.
   the bush   houseboy   sergeant
   Finish these sentences:
   The . . . . . was arrested for murder, by the . . . . . . When he was found,
   he was hiding in . . . . . .

After you read

3 Answer these questions:
   a Who kills Mary Turner?
   b Who calls for the police?
   c Why had Charlie Slatter come to Africa?
   d Who finds Mary Turner's body? Where?
   e Why has Tony Marston come to Africa?
   f Why don't Charlie Slatter and the Sergeant want to listen to Tony's
      'ideas' about the murder?
   g What happens to Tony after the trial?
   h Why does Mary choose to live in a girls' club when she leaves
      home to work in town?
   i How does Mary find out what her friends think about her?
   j How old is Mary when she decides to find someone to marry?
   k Where does Dick first see Mary?

Chapters 3–4

Before you read

4 What do you think Mary will find when she arrives at the farm? Will it
   be what she is expecting?

5 Make sure you understand the meaning of the word *candle*.
Now write a sentence using this group of words:
match/candle/suddenly

After you read

6 Dick says: 'This is the new missus.'
  a Who is he talking to?
  b Who is he talking about?
7 Answer these questions:
  a What does Dick's farmhouse remind Mary of?
  b How does Mary feel about Samson?
  c What is the understanding between Dick and Samson?
  d What is the first thing Mary learns?
  e What things does Mary do to fill the time?
  f Why does Samson leave his job?
  g How does Mary offend Mrs Slatter?
  h What does Charlie suggest to Dick?
8 Describe the way Mary treats the servants.

Chapters 5–6

Before you read

  9 How do you think Dick can help Mary to be happier with their life on the farm?
10 What would you do in Mary's situation?
11 Do you think the Slatters can do anything to help Dick and Mary? If so, what?
12 Check the meanings of these words in your dictionary:
beehive frost malaria turkey
  a Which one is a disease common in hot countries?
  b Which one do you only see in cold weather?
  c Write two sentences about Dick, using the words bees/beehives/failure/turkeys

After you read
13 Explain why Mary starts to think Dick might not succeed as a farmer.

14 Mary is very happy when she arrives in town. Explain what happens to change the way she feels.

15 Answer these questions:

   a What ideas does Dick waste money on?

   b Why is Mary unhappy about the shop?

   c Why does Mary take the whip with her when she goes out to the farm?

   d What does she find out while Dick is ill?

   e Why does Mary whip the farm worker?

   f Dick realises Mary is right about the farm but he is unhappy about following her ideas. Why?

Chapters 7–8

Before you read

16 Do you think Dick will succeed with the tobacco crop? Why or why not?

17 What do you think will happen next to change Mary's life?

After you read

18 Answer these questions:

   a What happens to the tobacco crop?

   b What makes Mary depressed?

   c Why does Dick say they can't have children?

   d Why does Dick bring Moses up to the house to be their servant?

   e What is Mary afraid of?

   f How does Moses behave towards Mary?

   g How does Mary feel after she has seen Moses washing?

   h Why is Dick angry with Mary?

   i What is the 'battle' that is happening in the house?

   j What happens when Moses tells Mary he is going to leave?

   k What does Mary feel about Moses now?

   l Moses behaviour towards Mary has changed. How?

Chapters 9–10

Before you read

19 Check the meaning of the word *earrings* in your dictionary. Make a sentence using these words:

gold/diamond/earrings/birthday

20 We already know the end of this story. What do you think happens to cause the murder?

After you read

21 How do other farmers in the area know about Dick and Mary?

22 Why is Charlie Slatter interested in the Turners?

23 Dick's farm hasn't been successful, but Charlie has made a lot of money out of his. But in some ways Dick is a better farmer than Charlie. Explain how.

24 Charlie hasn't visited the Turners for nearly two years. Describe the changes he sees in Mary and the house.

25 Answer these questions:

a What is Charlie given for supper?

b What surprises Charlie about Mary and Moses?

c What does Charlie suggest Dick should do?

d What does Tony think of Mary?

e Why is Tony afraid of Moses?

f On the morning of her last day, what makes Mary feel calm?

g Why do you think Mary says to herself, 'I don't understand'?

h How does Moses kill Mary?

Writing

26 'Doris Lessing paints a picture of life in Africa that can only be understood by white people who have lived there.' How true do you think this is? Why is it difficult for other people to understand the Africa Mary Turner knew?

27 Describe the house in which the Turners live. What changes does Mary make to it when she first arrives there? What do you imagine happens to the house after Mary dies?

28 Mary's life on the farm is very different from her life-style in town. Write a letter from Mary to one of the girls she used to work with. Tell her about a typical day on the farm.

29 When the news about Mary's murder reaches the town, people who knew her are very shocked. Write a conversation between some of the people Mary worked with.

30 The newspaper reports that Mary was killed during a robbery, but we know this isn't true. Write another report for the newspaper, after the first day of Moses' trial. Describe what happened in the court, and what was said.

31 This story is written in the third person. How is that useful to the writer? If you had to rewrite the last two chapters of the book in the first person which character would you choose to tell the story and why?